THE BLOT: LITTLE CITY CAT

THE BLOT:

LITTLE
CITY CAT

BY PHYLLIS CRAWFORD

ILLUSTRATED BY BARBARA COONEY

jC858bl

NEW YORK · HENRY HOLT & COMPANY

DESIGNED BY PAUL McPHARLIN

PRINTED IN THE UNITED STATES OF AMERICA

TO A LITTLE BOY NAMED

CELSUS

PRICE

PERRIE

PHILLIPS

THE BLOT: LITTLE CITY CAT

THE BLOT: LITTLE CITY CAT

Every morning when old Mr. Brindle unlocked the door of his little news-stand in the city, a little black cat was waiting for him just inside.

The little cat was black all over, so that sometimes Mr. Brindle took him for a shadow and almost stepped on him. Most of the time, though, he looked like a big blot of black ink. In fact, his name was The Blot.

The first thing Mr. Brindle did in the morning was to give The Blot his milk out of a saucer. Then The Blot was very busy drinking for a while—lap, lap, lap. Afterward, he was busy washing his face and paws and neck and ears.

That gave Mr. Brindle a chance to untie the bundles of new magazines and newspapers, and straighten up the little shop for the day. For if The Blot were not busy, he would get in Mr. Brindle's way. He would bite the corners of the papers, pull at the strings with his teeth while Mr. Brindle was trying to untie them, or grab at Mr. Brindle's hands, kicking and pretending to bite hard.

There was not very much room in the store. It was large enough for shelves all around the walls to hold magazines and papers, and there was a counter with a stool behind it for Mr. Brindle. There was just enough space left for a little cat and Mr. Brindle and two or three customers if they were not too fat.

All day Mr. Brindle sat on the stool behind the counter and sold papers and magazines to the customers. The Blot played with a string or with a piece of paper, or else he walked along the piles of magazines. Sometimes he hid behind the magazines and jumped out fiercely with shining eyes. Once he tore a big piece of paper into bits with his teeth, and Mr. Brindle had to clean up the bits.

Sometimes he got very tired and had to go to sleep. He could sleep anywhere, but he liked best to sleep on Mr. Brindle's knee. When The Blot was asleep on Mr. Brindle's knee, the customers had to help themselves, for he would not get up for anybody.

Mr. Brindle did often disturb The Blot when he was asleep, but petting him was different. The Blot liked to be petted, even when he was waked from sleep. When he was waked, he made a funny little noise like purring out loud, "Prrr-r-rrp!" And then he always purred under his breath as long as Mr. Brindle petted him.

Every day was almost the same as every other day. Mr. Brindle came in the morning and never left all day. He had his lunch in a bag, and The Blot had milk in his saucer. Sometimes The Blot had a dish of cold vegetables, which Mr. Brindle brought from home. And sometimes there was a bit of green grass or sorrel for his health.

Then every night Mr. Brindle went home, leaving The Blot in the store. The Blot sat inside the door watching the people go by for a while, and then he curled up on an old sweater on the floor behind the counter, and went to sleep.

THIS IS WHAT HAPPENED AT THE
NEWS-STAND ONE DAY

2

One morning The Blot sat at the door waiting and waiting for Mr.
Brindle long after the old man usually came. He got hungrier
and hungrier, and no one at all came. Customers stopped and
looked in and tried the door, and then went away. The Blot
meowed to them, but they seemed not to hear him.

After a long time, another man, named Mr. Pandle, came and unlocked the door, and took in the new magazines and newspapers. He had no bottle of milk, and he paid no attention to the little black cat.

The Blot went and sat in a corner and watched Mr. Pandle. His eyes followed Mr. Pandle all around.

When customers began to come in, they asked about Mr. Brindle. Mr. Pandle told them that Mr. Brindle was sick. He was taking care of the store until Mr. Brindle got well.

But still Mr. Pandle did not take care of the little black cat. He gave him no milk and no fresh water.

Finally The Blot went to his empty dish behind the counter, and meowed. Instead of feeding him, Mr. Pandle said, "Scat!" And he chased The Blot out of the store with the broom.

14

The Blot ran out on the sidewalk. He was frightened by the noise and the hurrying, and he had to jump to keep out of the way of the feet of the passers-by. His heart was pounding with fright.

And so he tried to go back into the news-stand whenever a customer opened the door. But Mr. Pandle chased him out every time. The Blot tried again and again, and was pushed or kicked out as often as he tried.

Finally he sat down on the sidewalk close against the wall beside the door, and cried, "Meow! meow!" He was hungry and he wanted his breakfast.

That time Mr. Pandle came out with the broom and chased The Blot halfway down the block. The little black cat had no place to go, but he had to run anyway.

THIS IS WHAT HAPPENED FIRST AFTER
THE BLOT LEFT THE NEWS-STAND

The Blot ran a little while, and then he walked a little while, and then he sat down and meowed a little while. And nothing happened.

So he walked a little while longer, straight down the street. It must have been almost time for lunch, and he had not had breakfast yet. He was almost too hungry to meow very loudly now.

After a while just ahead he saw a big gray cat balancing himself on the rim of an ash can. The gray cat was reaching in the ash can with one paw. As The Blot came nearer, the big cat fished out a bone and jumped down on the sidewalk with it.

The Blot was so glad to see the bone that he ran up to the big gray cat purring. But the big one took his bone in his mouth, growled and cuffed The Blot, and walked away to eat the bone somewhere else.

The Blot stood a moment watching him go. He was not purring any longer. He looked up at the ash can, and tried to reach the top by standing on his hind legs. But it was too high and he could not reach very far. Then he tried to jump up on the rim of the ash can as the other cat had done. Usually he could jump very well for such a little cat, but this time he was too hungry and too excited to jump high enough. He fell back every time he tried.

And so he had to give up trying to get a bone for himself out of that ash can. He ran down the street looking for the big gray cat with the bone. But he never, never found him, or the bone.

18

He kept on going down the street, and finally he did see another bone lying on the sidewalk near another ash can. He began to purr and ran very fast to get the bone before anyone else saw it. But just as he reached it and put one paw on it, a big dirty white cat with a scratch on his nose came. The white cat wrinkled up his scratched nose and growled, and looked at The Blot angrily.

At that, The Blot ran away without saying a word. He kept on running down the street.

THIS IS WHAT HAPPENED AFTER THE BLOT PASSED THE ASH CANS

4

While The Blot was running down the street it began to rain. A big drop of rain fell on his nose, and another drop fell on his left ear, and another on his right ear. Rain fell on his fur all over. He shook himself all over, but the rain kept falling, and he got wetter and wetter.

He tried to get away from the rain by crouching against the side of a building, but the rain came down slanting, and he got wetter and wetter still. His ears drooped, and water trickled down his nose. He was shivering, too. He cried very hoarsely, "Meow! meow! meow!"

Then he started walking down the street again. He might as well get wet looking for food and a dry place as staying in one spot.

In a little while he came to an open door. It was the door of a grocery store, and it was dry and warm inside. The Blot went in and hid behind a box.

The grocery store was dry and warm.

He shook one foot and he shook another foot, and he shook another foot and another, until he had shaken the water off all his feet. Then he sat down and shivered.

When he began to get warmer, he began to wash himself. You might think that after he had got so wet, he would be clean enough. Besides, being a black cat, it would not show if he were dirty.

Just the same, he gave himself a bath. He licked his forepaws very carefully, and washed his face and his ears by scrubbing with his forepaws. He licked himself all over, smoothing down his wet fur neatly. Some places were hard to reach. When he had finished, he curled up in a round damp ball, and went to sleep. He was so tired that he slept for a long time.

When he woke up, he was hungrier than ever. He walked out from behind his box, and explored the grocery store, smelling things. He found a pile of small sardine cans. They smelled like fish and had a little oil and sawdust on the outside. He licked at the oil, but some of the sawdust got in his mouth and choked him. He had to cough.

He saw boxes and baskets of fresh vegetables. One box had

22

spinach in it. He took a bite of the spinach. The grocer was looking, though, and did not want him to eat the spinach. The grocer picked The Blot up by the tail and dropped him behind the counter. The little black cat cried out, because it hurt him to be held by the tail.

"Where did this kitten come from?" the grocer asked the clerk.

"I don't know. I never saw him before," answered the clerk.

"Well, don't feed him, and he won't stay," said the grocer. "We don't need a cat."

The little cat stayed behind the counter where he had been put, and looked for food there. He found nothing good. He did find a grape and he tried to eat it, but it was not good.

Then someone dropped a big pasteboard box behind the counter, and it fell on The Blot's tail. It frightened him so that he ran out of the grocery store to the sidewalk.

But it was still raining outside. When The Blot saw that, and felt the rain on his fur, he started to run back into the store. But just then the clerk began to sweep in the doorway with a big broom. He swept out the dirt, and he swept out bits of spinach and lettuce and celery that had fallen on the floor. He swept the floor clean. And he swept the little black cat right away from the door.

THIS IS WHAT HAPPENED AFTER
THE BLOT LEFT THE GROCERY STORE

5

And so The Blot had to run out of the grocery store into the rain again. He was not so much afraid of the people on the sidewalk now, for he was more used to them and could dodge their feet more easily.

He ran very fast until he saw another lighted doorway. But this was not the doorway of a store. It was an apartment house, and the door was shut.

It looked warm inside the hallway of the apartment house. He could see the hallway through the glass door. He sat down on the sidewalk beside the door and meowed. He meowed until a young lady in a blue hat came down the street and turned in at this door.

"Oh, the poor little kitten!" she said, and stooped and picked him up. He was very wet, but she did not mind that.

She was taking him into the hallway, but the elevator man stopped her. "I'm sorry, ma'am," said the elevator man. "No cats are allowed in this building. He'll have to go out."

The young lady had to put The Blot out into the rain again. She did not want to do that, and she gave him a good petting and told him good-bye. The Blot sat down and meowed at the door again, but nobody paid any attention to him.

26

Finally he left the apartment house doorway and ran down the street in the rain, looking for another open door. He looked and looked, and ran and ran. But there were no more lighted doorways opening on the sidewalk. The houses along here had steps leading up to the front door, long high steps.

Just as The Blot was passing one of the houses, he saw someone come out of the front door at the top of the steps. He tried to hop up the steps and get inside before the door closed, but he was too late. He sat down at the closed door and meowed. In a little while a woman opened the door and said, "Scat!" She pushed The Blot away with a broom, and he had to run down the steps to the street.

Now that he knew the way up the steps into houses like this, The Blot tried the house next door. He hopped up the steps and meowed loudly with his cold wet nose against the crack of the door. He meowed and meowed. But after he had meowed a little while, he began to wrinkle his nose and sniff. There was a smell of dog about that door, and he did not like it at all.

And so he ran down the steps to the sidewalk.

28

THIS IS WHAT HAPPENED AFTER
THE BLOT HAD TRIED TWO HOUSES

Then The Blot tried the house next door to the one with the dog smell. At *this* door, he had no sooner begun to meow than the door opened, and a little girl named Anne Alexander looked out.

When she saw that it was a little black cat who had come to see her, she squealed and picked him up in her arms. She did not mind his being wet either. She rubbed her chin against his head, and he purred very loudly.

Anne carried him in to show to her mother, and asked if she might keep him.

"No, dear," said her mother. "He is only a stray cat. Besides, I don't think we need a cat."

"Oh, please, mother," begged Anne. "I need a cat."

Mrs. Alexander shook her head. That meant *no*, and begging would not help. But Anne did want to keep the little cat.

"Well, then, mother, may I give him some milk and keep him until he is dry and warm, and until it has stopped raining?"

"Yes, you may do that," said her mother.

Anne took The Blot into the kitchen, and poured some milk into a saucer. The little cat got so excited that he tried to drink the milk as it was being poured. When Anne stopped pouring, he began to lap the milk greedily. He was in such a hurry that he gulped.

He drank every drop of the milk, and had a second helping. Then he sat down to wash himself all over once more, beginning by licking the corners of his mouth with his pink tongue. When he was all clean, he sighed and curled up for a nap.

Anne had been watching him all the time, but she did not disturb him, either when he was drinking his milk or after he had gone to sleep. And so The Blot slept and slept, curled up in a tight ball beside the empty saucer.

7

The tired little black cat kept on sleeping for a long time, and it kept on raining outside. Anne left The Blot alone in the kitchen, but she tiptoed in to see him often. The Blot slept and slept.

After a while, however, Mary the cook began rattling pots and pans, getting dinner. The noise waked The Blot, and he was interested in everything she did. He had never watched anyone preparing a meal before.

He followed Mary around the kitchen, and stood on his hind legs sometimes to try to see into the pans. When she began to fix a chicken he smelled it and saw it, and he meowed and meowed. She reminded him that he had had two saucerfuls of milk, but he kept on meowing. Finally to keep him quiet she gave him the neck of the chicken.

Instead of eating it, The Blot took the piece of meat in his mouth and carried it to the door. As soon as the door was

32

She gave him the neck of the chicken.

opened he ran into the house with it. He ran until he found Anne in the living room.

He ran up to her, meowing. And when a cat meows with his mouth full, it is almost as funny as when people talk with their mouths full. The Blot said, "Mrow-row-row!" He sounded so funny that Anne laughed.

He laid the piece of meat on the floor at Anne's feet and looked up at her, purring. But Anne did not pick up the meat. She did not want it. The Blot purred and rubbed against her feet and meowed several times and said, "Prrr-r-rrp!"

When he saw that Anne was not going to eat the piece of meat, he took it behind the sofa and ate it himself. Someone had to eat it. He made a lot of noise when he ate. He cracked the bones and smacked. Now and then he would stop to look up at Anne and purr.

Anne said, "Little black cat, you must not make so much noise when you eat."

But cats are not supposed to know how to eat quietly, like people. So The Blot kept on eating noisily until he had finished.

34

THIS IS WHAT HAPPENED AT DINNER
TIME AT ANNE'S HOUSE

Then came dinner time. Mr. Alexander had come home from his office, and it was evening.

While Anne and her father and mother were in the dining room having dinner, The Blot discovered a game that he could play by himself. He played it in the living room where the floor was smoothest. He played the game with a small rug.

He ran across the floor—scratch, scratch, scratch! All the way across the room he scampered, and then jumped on the small rug and slid with it.

He ran and slid on the rug until he got tired of that, and then he rolled over and over, biting and kicking the corner of the rug. He held it tightly with his forepaws and kicked with his hind paws.

He got the rug so mussed up that he could crawl under it. He hid underneath the rug, peeping out now and then with big shining eyes to see if anyone were coming. He patted at the floor, poking his black paws out from his hiding place under the rug.

Then he came out and scampered around the room. He sharpened his claws on the big rug once. Then he went back underneath the small rug to hide.

After dinner, Anne looked and looked for The Blot. She looked in the kitchen, and she looked in the dining room. She looked in the hall, and finally she looked in the living room. But she could not see him anywhere, and he did not answer or come when she called him.

Then she noticed that the little rug was mussed up. She knew at once where The Blot was. He was hiding, and keeping very still.

36

She put her hand under the little rug, and The Blot grabbed
her hand with his paws, and pretended to bite her.

"You are a bad cat, to hide from me," said Anne.

But she did not spank him. Instead, she helped him play by
poking pieces of paper into his hiding place for him to bite and
chew.

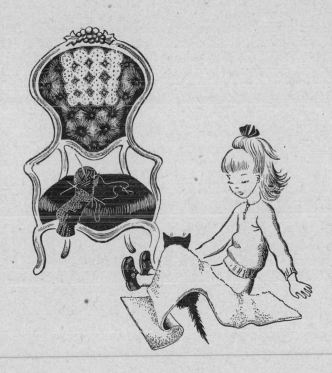

THIS IS WHAT HAPPENED AT ANNE'S HOUSE AFTER DINNER

9

Then before anyone realized how late it was, it was time for Anne to go to bed. It was still raining outside, and so The Blot had to stay all night.

Anne got a box for the little cat to sleep in, and put some soft rags in it for a bed. She put the box in the kitchen near the stove so that he could be warm.

Then she put The Blot to bed in his box, and said good night to him. But as soon as she started to leave the kitchen, he jumped right out of the box and followed her to the door. She picked him up and put him back in the box and started to leave him again. Again he hopped out of his box and ran after her. This happened again and again—at least six times, and maybe more.

And all the time, Mrs. Alexander kept telling Anne to hurry to bed. Finally Anne had to slip out of the kitchen door and shut it in a hurry before The Blot could get out.

38

The Blot sat at the door in the kitchen and meowed and meowed at first. But after a while he stopped meowing and curled up on the floor under the stove. He slept all night long, except for a while when he woke up and walked around the kitchen looking at everything and smelling everything he could reach.

THIS IS WHAT HAPPENED THE NEXT
MORNING AT ANNE'S HOUSE

10

Almost as soon as it was day, Anne came downstairs to see The Blot and play with him. As soon as he saw her he said, "Prrr-r-rrp!" He rubbed and rubbed against her ankles.

She sat down on the floor beside him while he drank his milk for breakfast. She wanted to pet him every minute, but every time she touched him, he stopped drinking his milk, and purred and politely hoisted his tail. He could not eat his breakfast very well so long as she disturbed him. So she finally left him alone, and just watched.

As soon as he had finished, and had washed himself with his tongue very carefully, Anne took him into the living room to play with him. She made a piece of paper into a ball, and tied it on a string. She went up and down the room, trailing the ball on the floor.

At first The Blot just watched her. But after a little while his eyes began to shine, and he crouched down flat on the floor. He switched his tail and wriggled, and then he jumped at the paper ball.

He bit the ball and held it tightly with his forepaws while he kicked hard with his hind paws. He held on so that Anne could not pull it away from him. Then he let go suddenly, and she was pulling so hard on the string that she almost fell down.

Then she gave him a paper ball without a string attached. He took his ball in his mouth and carried it about the room. He

threw the ball up with a toss of his head, and then jumped on it
as it came down. He grabbed it in his mouth again, and growled
funny little high-pitched growls.

Then he dropped the ball and walked away as if he did not like
it any longer. But when he was several feet away from it, he
turned and ran back to jump on it again, and knocked it about
with his paws. He jumped on it again and slid on it, growling and
growling.

THIS IS WHAT HAPPENED AFTER THE BLOT
PLAYED WITH THE PAPER BALL

11

When Mrs. Alexander came downstairs to breakfast that morning, Anne showed her how much fun The Blot was having with his paper ball.

"Now may I keep him?" she asked.

"No, dear, not even now," said her mother. "We will find another home for him."

Anne cried then, for she did want to have a little black cat. But crying did no good, and so she stopped, and had breakfast with her father and mother.

While they were having breakfast, The Blot wandered off by himself, smelling the furniture and rugs and doors. That was the way he made himself at home.

He went upstairs, and walked into Anne's room. He first sharpened his claws on the leg of the table. Table legs are much better than rugs for sharpening claws. When his claws were sharp enough, The Blot looked up at the table. It was rather

43

high. But there was a chair not far away, to which he could easily jump. He went from the floor to the chair and from the chair to the table without once bending his knees to get a good jump. He was feeling better than he had the day before, and looked very proud of the way he could jump.

On the table were several picture books. He smelled them, but he did not seem to like them.

Then he saw a little white goose with yellow feet and a yellow bill, made of china. That was nice and shiny. He smelled it, and it was so cold against his nose that he sneezed.

He patted the little china goose with one paw, and then he patted it with the other paw. He moved the little china goose a tiny bit. He kept on patting it with first one paw and then the other, until it fell off the table. It broke in pieces on the floor.

The Blot looked surprised, and leaned over the edge of the table to look at the pieces.

Just then Anne came into the room. She had been looking for him all over the house. When she saw what he had done, she said, "Oh, you bad cat! Now I must spank you."

The Blot did not like the tone of her voice, and so he jumped down from the table and ran out of the room. He ran down the hall, and hid under the bed in Mrs. Alexander's room.

Anne looked and looked for him. She looked even under her mother's bed, but he was so black that she could not see him. He sat very still, and watched her looking for him.

After a while, though, he got tired of sitting still. He came out, and yawned, and stretched his front legs and his hind legs and shook himself.

By that time Anne had decided not to spank him. She did not even tell her mother about the china goose, for fear of losing The Blot.

He hid under the bed in Mrs. Alexander's room.

THIS IS WHAT HAPPENED AFTER THE BLOT BROKE THE CHINA GOOSE

12

A little while later, while Anne was cleaning up her room, The Blot went around by himself looking for something else to do. He went into Mrs. Alexander's room again.

On the window sill in the sunlight he saw a pot with pink begonias growing in it. Now The Blot had not had anything green to eat in a long time, except the bite of spinach in the grocery store. He did like a bit of green once in a while, and besides, it was good for him. And so when he saw the plant on the window sill he ran over and jumped up beside it on the sill.

The flowers were very pink, and the leaves green and shiny. He smelled both the flowers and the leaves. He nibbled a leaf. It had a sour taste, like sorrel, and it crunched when he chewed it. He ate a whole leaf, and another, and another. They were not very big leaves.

Then he sat looking out of the window for a while. All he could see was little bare back yards, and nothing happening in

47

48

them. There was not even a fly on the screen for him to chase.

So he looked at the begonia plant again, and took another bite. He ate a whole leaf, and another. It was not long before almost all the leaves were gone, and The Blot ate most of the flowers too. The flowers tasted almost the same as the leaves. When he got tired of eating the begonia plant, there was nothing left of it except the stalks and a few leaves. Then The Blot began to nose around in the soil in the pot. After a while he wandered away.

When Anne's mother came into her room later, she found her flower plant nearly bare. She said, "Oh, dear! Insects must have got into my flowers and eaten them up."

But she could not find any insects at all.

Maybe no one would have known who ate the begonias if The Blot had washed all the earth off his whiskers. But Mrs. Alexander saw his dirty whiskers, and then she knew. She scolded him.

"We must get rid of this cat at once," she said.

THIS IS WHAT HAPPENED AFTER THE BLOT
ATE THE BEGONIAS

13

After scolding The Blot about the flowers, Mrs. Alexander put him in the kitchen and shut the door. She told Anne not to play with him, because he had been a bad cat, and should be punished. The Blot meowed and scratched at the kitchen door to get out, but no one paid any attention to him.

And when the grocer's boy came with the groceries, Mrs. Alexander gave him The Blot and asked him to find a home for the little cat. The grocer's boy carried him away under his arm.

And so The Blot rode away in a big truck with the grocer's boy. It was not very far up the street, but the little cat was frightened, and scratched the boy trying to get away. The Blot struggled and struggled to get away, but he was held too tightly.

When they came to the grocery store, the boy took The Blot to the grocer and asked what he should do with him.

"That looks like the same stray kitten that came in here yesterday," said the grocer. And of course it was the same

50

kitten, for this was the same grocer who had picked The Blot up by the tail when he nibbled at the spinach.

"Put him down," said the grocer. "We can find someone to take him away."

The boy put The Blot down on the floor, and the little cat walked around the store smelling a few cans and boxes. He saw the spinach in the boxes on the floor, and started toward it. Then he looked at the grocer, laid his ears back, and walked away in another direction.

51

He went behind the counter, and saw a pasteboard box there, like the one that had fallen on his tail. His ears twitched and the tip of his tail twitched. Maybe he did not like the look of that box.

He walked out from behind the counter. Just then the clerk took a broom and began to sweep—swish, swish, swish. That sound did not please the Blot at all. He had been chased away with a broom too often in the last two days.

When the clerk began to sweep toward him, The Blot ran out of the grocery store as fast as he could run. No one had to take him away, for he took himself away.

THIS IS WHAT HAPPENED AFTER THE BLOT LEFT THE GROCERY STORE THE SECOND TIME

14

The Blot ran out of the grocery store, and he ran up the street as hard as he could run. He ran and he ran and he ran, straight up the street. He passed men's feet and children's feet and women's feet hurrying one way or another. He passed ash cans and ash cans. He passed a big dirty white cat and he passed a great gray cat. He passed everything. Oh, he was running!

The first thing he knew, there was a familiar doorway, and someone coming out with a newspaper under his arm. The Blot ran up to the doorway, and stopped just long enough to smell the door to be certain that it was the right place. Then he began to scratch at the crack of the door, and to say, "Meow! meow! meow!"

The door opened in a hurry, for it was the door of the news-stand. And there was Mr. Brindle himself, not sick any longer. He was there to sell newspapers and magazines as usual.

Mr. Brindle took The Blot up in his arms.

54

Mr. Brindle took The Blot up in his arms and rubbed his chin against the black fur, and was very happy.

"I brought some milk for my little cat when I came back this morning," said Mr. Brindle to The Blot, "and when I got here, there was no little black cat. I am glad you came back. Will you have your milk now?"

The Blot purred and purred, and rubbed against Mr. Brindle. When Mr. Brindle poured his milk into his saucer, The Blot lapped it up very, very fast, washed his face and paws and neck and ears, and then jumped up on Mr. Brindle's knee for a nap. He went to sleep purring.

While The Blot was sleeping on his knee, Mr. Brindle would not get up for anybody, and his customers had to help themselves. Mr. Brindle petted The Blot now and then while he lay on his knee, and The Blot had to wake up and purr for him again.

When The Blot had finished his nap, he got up and yawned and stretched, and he almost sharpened his claws on Mr. Brindle's knee. He remembered just in time that it was Mr. Brindle.

He jumped down and went over to a pile of newspapers on the bottom shelf. He began biting at the corners of the papers and trying to tear off bits with his teeth. Mr. Brindle called to him to stop, because the customers would not want torn papers. Then The Blot hid behind the pile of papers and jumped out at Mr. Brindle with shining eyes.

He found a piece of string, and carried it around in his mouth for a while, getting all tangled up in it. He lay down on the floor and played with it.

He was playing just as he used to play before Mr. Pandle chased him away the day when Mr. Brindle was sick.

And you might have thought that The Blot had never been away at all.